THE Little Witch's BIRTHDAY PARTY

Written by **Michael Pellico**

Illustrated by Christina Berry

See more children's books by Moonbow Publishing at:
https://MoonbowPublishing.com

First Print Edition
ISBN 978-1-7339130-5-8
Library of Congress Control Number: 2020907857
Printed in USA

This book is dedicated to:
Sabrina Pellico
The inspiration for this story...
and many others.

And to my mother:
Helen Pellico
My hero and guiding light
throughout my life.

It was a beautiful spring day. Sabrina was lying in her hammock looking up at the puffy passing clouds, imagining what shapes they looked like. On her lap was Snowball, her Maltese puppy friend.

"Snowball, we have only two weeks to prepare for Anna's first ever birthday party." Anna was the little witch Sabrina rescued from a tree, when she had dropped her broom and could not fly away. Anna had told Sabrina she had never had a birthday party, and Sabrina was determined to have a big party for her. However, she had never thrown a party for a witch before!

Snowball looked at Sabrina and seemed to understand what she was saying. Sabrina talked to Snowball about everything. Telling Snowball her problems made them much easier to solve.

"I think we will have red velvet cake, ice cream, fried chicken, and pizza, with lots of yummy toppings. Maybe sushi too. I love sushi! Anna told me she never had ice cream or cake. I wonder what flavor ice cream she likes. Chocolate? Strawberry? With lots of whipped cream? And a cherry on top?!" Snowball smiled, and so did Sabrina. Sabrina already told her friends about the big party, and they were so excited to meet Anna. They had never met a real witch before.

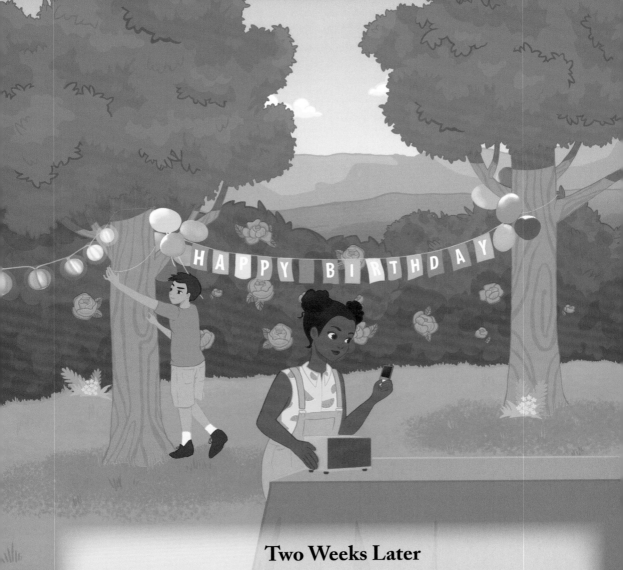

Two Weeks Later

Sabrina, her younger brother Stephen, and her best friend Mikayla were decorating Sabrina's backyard. They were busy hanging colorful balloons and a big "HAPPY BIRTHDAY" banner. They set the table with party dishes, cups, and a matching tablecloth.

"I really like the twinkle lights we put up," said Stephen. "They look so colorful. Mikayla, did you remember to bring the birthday party music?"

3

"I sure did!" Mikayla replied, with a smile.

"Now remember, I did not tell my parents that Anna is a real witch. They probably would not believe me anyway. My mom keeps asking how I know her, and I said we met during Halloween," Sabrina told her.

"Well, I told my mom," she just laughed and said, "that's nice and walked away! I am sure she did not believe me!" said Mikayla, who then looked up and said excitedly, "here comes Billy and Audrey!"

4

Billy, a shy boy, and his sister, Audrey, were Sabrina's next-door neighbors. They often had fun sleep overs with Sabrina and Stephen, where they stayed up late playing games and ate popcorn. Soon the other children started to arrive. Susan, who was eleven, loved to sing.

Mary, a mischievous girl, loved to play imaginary games with Sabrina and make up stories of adventure.

Helen, and her sister Pam, were identical twins. No one could tell them apart, and sometimes they even switched places!

Ilona was nine and a half years old and was always laughing. She was never in a bad mood. She would make

Sabrina laugh whenever she was sad.

Julie, Rachel, Emma, Donnie, and Paulie were next to arrive. They were all Sabrina's classmates.

The children brought lots of presents and put them on the small decorated table. Everyone was so excited and could not wait to meet Anna.

"Did anyone tell their parents that Anna is a real witch?" Sabrina asked.

All the children raised their hands. "Yes," many said, while others nodded in agreement.

Helen smiled as she said, "My mom did not believe Pam and me. She just laughed and told us to have a great time."

"Mine did the same," exclaimed Ilona.

"Mine too," said Rachel. All the children giggled.

Suddenly there was a whooshing sound from above. The children looked up as Anna slowly descended on her broom. Her cat sat calmly and looked at all the wide-eyed children staring at them. About a foot off of the ground, the broom stopped and Anna hopped off. Her cat leaped to the ground and curled around Anna's legs. Anna was wearing a beautiful purple dress, with a black hat that had a blue band around it. In the center of that hat, was a small silver star.

Anna looked a little nervous, but she smiled when Sabrina ran up to her. Sabrina gave her a big hug, grabbed her hand excitedly, and said, "I am so happy you are here! This is your first birthday party ever and we will have so much fun!"

"I am so excited to be here," Anna replied, as she gave her new friend another hug. She looked down at her white cat, "This is Aurora. I always talk to her, and she understands me. When I told her I was coming here, she jumped up on my broom. Aurora is named after the lights we see in the night sky."

"Wow!" Sabrina exclaimed, "We call those lights the aurora borealis or the northern lights."

Sabrina picked up Snowball, laughed, and said, "Snowball also understands what I say or think. When I have big decisions, I always talk to her, and the way she acts helps me decide what to do. She helped me plan your party."

Sabrina put Snowball down. The Maltese ran over to Aurora and placed her paw on the cat. Sabrina and Anna laughed as they watched the two wag their tails and circle around happily, getting to know each other.

"They are already good friends," Anna said happily. "Good," said Sabrina, "they can run around the yard enjoying themselves. Maybe Snowball will introduce Aurora to my rabbit, Rabby, who also lives here."

"You have a rabbit too?" Anna asked, "You are so lucky!"

"You can come here and play with Snowball and Rabby any time you want. Now come and meet my friends. They are so happy to meet you!

"Everyone come here and meet Anna!" Sabrina called. All the children ran over to them, and somewhat shyly, started introducing themselves.

"Hi! I am Mikayla. I just had my birthday last month. Are you really a witch?"

Anna laughed and said, "Yes, I am."

10

11

"I love your clothes." Mikayla said, "Where did you buy such beautiful clothes?"

"My mother makes them for me with magic."

"Wow! That is so cool!" said Emma, "Your mother is a witch too?"

Anna laughed, "Of course my mother is a witch and so is my brother."

"You have a brother?" asked Julie.

"Yes, I do," said Anna, "he is a year older than me. He wanted to come to my party, but I did not know if he was invited. Please let him come!"

"Oh yes! He can come. We want him here. We want him to enjoy your first birthday party too!" said Sabrina.

Anna was very happy and yelled, "Hooray! I will bring him here now. He will be so happy." Taking out her wand, Anna pointed to an empty space and said the magic words:

"Space, space,
where there be no door,
make a door.
A door, where my brother waits on the other side,
I implore."

A blue light flashed from her wand. Suddenly, a shimmering blue oval appeared. All the children gasped in amazement as a boy stepped through. He looked a little older than Anna and was dressed in green pants and a tan shirt, a red and black cape on his back. He had silver hair, gorgeous blue eyes, and a very big smile. On his arm sat a beautiful bird, a falcon!

Anna rushed up to her brother and hugged him tightly, "Come and meet all my new friends," Anna said, as she grabbed him by the hand and brought him over to the starry-eyed children. "This is my brother Drew. This is the first birthday party he has ever been to."

Stephen got closer to Drew and exclaimed, "Your bird is beautiful. Is he a falcon?"

"Oh yes," replied Drew, "this is Flash, he is a Peregrine Falcon and is one of the fastest birds on Earth."

"That's so awesome!" said Stephen, as he got an even closer look at Flash, "By the way, are you a witch too?"

Drew smiled and shook his head, "No, I am a warlock. Only girls can be witches. Boys are warlocks."

"Can you do magic?" asked Stephen, curiously.

"Of course," replied Drew.

Stephen's eyes grew wide as he said, "Wow, Anna! Your cat just changed colors! She is now purple!"

"Of course she can change colors," laughed Anna. That is how you can tell what mood she is in. Aurora can

13

change colors just like the lights in the sky. She changes color depending on her mood. If happy, Aurora is white. If angry, she is red. When she is sad, she turns a pretty blue. Sometimes Aurora is green, pink, or even silver. Don't your cats change color too?"

"No, they cannot," Stephen said sadly, while shaking his head.

"Can you make Snowball change color with magic?" Sabrina asked.

Anna gave a thoughtful look and replied, "I will ask my mother. She is a very powerful witch and knows more magical spells than I do. I am sure she has a special spell that will work."

Stephen turned to Drew, "Do you play basketball or ice skate or swim?"

Drew shook his head, "No, I never have."

"Well then, I will teach you!" Stephen replied, as he walked away waving his hand to Drew and the other boys. "Come over here and we will play basketball. Flash can watch."

"Sounds like fun!" Drew said, as he followed Stephen.

Shortly afterward, Sabrina's Mom called out, "All the food is ready, so come and get it. Hope everyone is hungry."

15

Sabrina's mom walked over and asked Sabrina to introduce her new friend.

"This is Anna. She is my new friend and a witch!" Sabrina said.

"Of course she is," Sabrina's mom said with a smile. She patted Sabrina on the head and walked away.

"Haha, she does not believe you are a real witch," Sabrina said.

Anna and Sabrina giggled and held hands as they walked to the table. There was fried chicken, pizza, with lots of toppings, macaroni and cheese, corn-on-the cob, and sushi!

Sabrina invited everyone to help themselves.

"Everything looks sooooo good," exclaimed Anna, "I am so happy and hungry."

18

The children got their dishes, picked out what they wanted to eat, and found a place to sit at the table. Anna had a big pile of food on her dish. "I can't decide what I want, so I will try everything," Anna said, as she sat at the middle of the table, as the guest of honor. On her left side was Sabrina, and to her right was Audrey. Drew sat at the end of the table with the other boys.

After they finished eating to their hearts content, Sabrina announced it was time for cake.

The birthday cake was amazing. Anna's eyes were smiling. The red velvet cake was covered in fluffy white frosting and sprinkled with green and silver sparkles. It was decorated with a picture of Anna and Aurora riding a broom over an oak tree. A number "8" candle was in the center, surrounded by eight multi-colored candles.

"I drew you and Aurora," Sabrina said, "and I hope you like it."

"I love it," exclaimed Anna, while hugging Sabrina. "My first birthday cake. Thank you, Sabrina, and I thank all of your friends for coming!"

"Let's light the candles and sing 'Happy Birthday' to Anna!" Sabrina called out, "Who has the matches?"

"Oh no, we forgot the matches," Mikayla said, sadly.

Unexpectedly, Drew stepped in laughing and said, "Do not worry." He took out his wand, pointed it toward the candles, and said,

"Candles, candles on Anna's cake,
light up, and sparkle,
sparkle great."

Suddenly, the candles popped and lit up with flames that looked like little sparklers. Laughing, Drew said, "I made them sparkle to be extra special."

The children were once again amazed. They all ran up to Drew and invited him to their next birthday party.

"You must come to my party," said the twins, in unison.

"Yes Drew, come to mine too," said Ilona. "It is next month on the 17th. Please!"

Everyone was clapping their hands. Drew laughed again, and replied, "I will try!"

"And bring your falcon!" yelled Donnie.

"You must," shouted Billy.

"Of course, I will. He always goes where I go!" replied Drew.

"Now let's sing 'Happy Birthday,'" exclaimed Stephen.

"Wait," Drew said thoughtfully, "I do not know the words."

Anna laughed and said to her brother, "Do not worry, I have a magical idea." She took out her wand, pointed it in the air, and said,

"Letters and words, words of a Happy Birthday song, appear. Appear in the air so we can all sing, sing a Happy Birthday song!!"

A shimmer appeared in front of the table, with the words of a song in bright, sparkly purple letters. Anna's favorite color!

"Yeah! Let's all sing," cried out Sabrina.

21

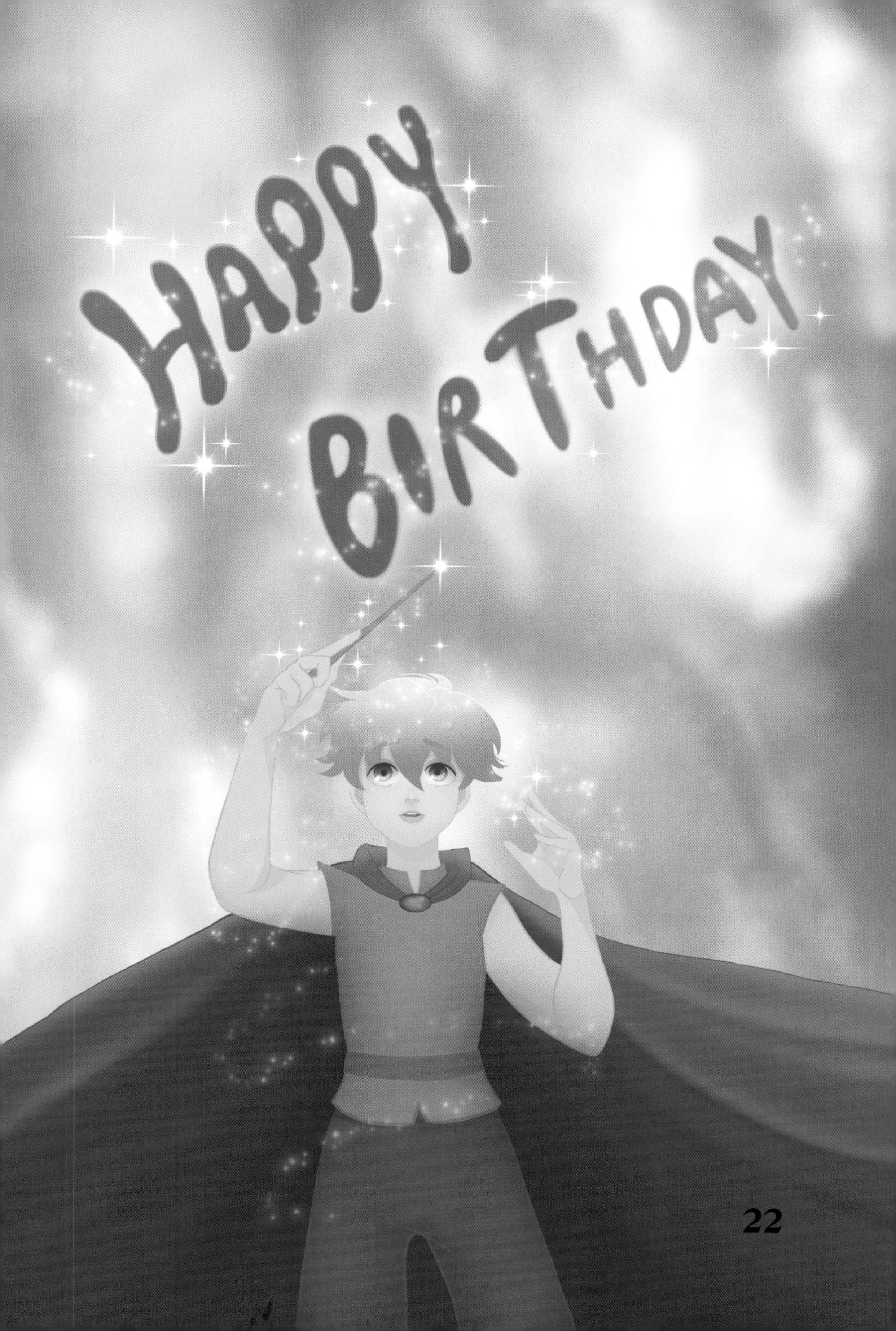
HAPPY
BIRTHDAY

All the children started singing a special 'Happy Birthday' song to Anna.

"Happy birthday to you. Happy birthday to our new friend, dear Anna, happy birthday to you. We wish you a happy, happy birthday and much happiness always, too!"

As soon as the last note was sung, the words faded away. Sabrina told Anna to make a wish and blow out the candles.

Anna made a wish and blew out the candles.

They all enjoyed the red velvet cake and ice cream. Anna especially loved the chocolate ice cream with whipped cream and a cherry on top! After dessert, Sabrina

announced, "Time for the Pumpkin Piñata."

Anna and Drew had never played this game before. All the children took turns, trying to hit the piñata while blindfolded. After the second time around, Audrey finally broke it and all the candy fell to the ground. The children ran to pick up as many pieces of candy as they could hold.

"Time for presents," Sabrina told Anna and the children.

They all gathered around the table filled with presents. Anna sat in a special chair, decorated with ribbons and bows. She was smiling. She had never seen so many colorfully decorated presents. Anna unwrapped her first present, it was a book on cats. The next present was a purple jump rope, followed by friendship bracelets, and silver necklace with a kitty charm. Then, Anna opened her last present, a pink, strawberry flavored lip gloss.

"Anna, I have a special present for you," Sabrina said, taking her by the hand.

Stephen carried out a large present, wrapped in blue paper with a big purple bow. Anna eagerly unwrapped the present and exclaimed, "It's a bicycle, a beautiful purple bicycle! I love it. Thank you so much. How did you know purple is my favorite color?"

Sabrina laughed, as she said, "Snowball helped me out, of course."

Anna also laughed, and then said, "I do not know how to ride a bicycle.

"Of course I will teach you," Sabrina replied.

"I will bring it to where I live. No one else has one!" Anna said, holding her new purple bicycle proudly. "I want to give you a gift as well," Anna continued, "I believe that the time and effort you put into making this party is far better than magic. All the planning, cooking, and everything—down to last detail. It showed me what a true friend you are. Now, I have a special present for you."

Anna found a twig on the ground and sticking it straight up into the dirt, she circled her hand above it, and said,

"Virga cresco volare!"

The twig began to vibrate and grow in size, taller and taller, as one end of the branch turned into bristles. In a matter of seconds, the twig became a broom.

"Sabrina, pick up the broom," Anna said. Sabrina walked forward and grasped the broom. "Now you are its

owner, and this magic broom will respond only to your touch."

"You mean, I can fly with it? Just like you?" asked Sabrina.

"Yes!" Anna said.

"Since I met you, I dreamed of flying! This means so much to me," said Sabrina. "I'd love to try it right now." They glanced around to see the kids nodding in excitement.

"Get on it," Anna told Sabrina. "You will not fall unless you hit a tree." As she laughed

Sabrina listened and climbed onto the broom. "Now, to control the broom, you need to lean left if you want to go left, and lean right if you want to go right. To go up, pull gently up. Push down, to go down. To go faster, say 'Faster.' To go slower, say, 'Slower.' Now let's go for a short ride. Remember what I told you, pull up gently and then hold steady."

Suddenly, Snowball jumped onto Sabrina's lap. "Do not worry, she cannot fall off. The broom will keep her safe!" Anna said.

Sabrina was thrilled! Speaking quietly, Sabrina said, "Forward," and she began to move, "Wow! This is so wonderful Anna!"

"You are a fast learner, Sabrina," Anna said, as she hopped on her broom and together they circled the yard, while the children below laughed and ran after them in amazement.

After a short time, they landed. As Sabrina got off the broom, she said, "I better not tell my parents, at least not right away. They will be too afraid to let me ride the broom."

"Good idea," replied Anna, "but now that you have a magic broom, you can visit where I live. Only by magic can you go there."

Then looking at the sky, Anna said, "It's getting dark. I must be going. This has been the best day of my life! I am so grateful. I will be back so I can ride my new bicycle with you. Drew will take it with him, so I can practice."

After hugging all her new friends and saying goodbye, Anna rose on her broom with a white-colored Aurora. With a big wave and smile, she disappeared into the beautiful, early evening sky.

Drew took the bicycle and presents, turned to the children, and said, "Thank you for inviting me to my sister's first birthday party. I hope we are forever friends." Pointing his wand, a blue shimmer appeared again. Drew, Flash, the purple bicycle, and all the other presents faded and disappeared.

Sabrina and her friends all agreed that this was the most exciting birthday party ever and started planning the next one.

Sabrina took her broom and hid it in the back of her bedroom closet. "Snowball, you and I are going to have so much fun flying around and exploring everywhere. However, we must be careful to not be seen."

It had been a long day. Sabrina got into bed with Snowball and was soon fast asleep, dreaming of the new adventures she would have when visiting the magical world where Anna lives!

The End

About the Author

Michael Pellico is a medical researcher, writer, and film producer. One of eleven children whose parents both worked long hours. It was his responsibility to help raise his siblings. Growing up "poor", he entertained them with stories, and later telling stories to their children. This book and all his stories are dedicated to Sabrina, his niece, who insists that he tell her a story each time they are together. We hope that you love them as much as Sabrina does!

About the Illustrator

Christina Berry is an established book artist who enjoys all types of mediums in illustration. She has spent much of her adult life pursuing a degree in Microbiology and working with special needs kids, but she changed course to her first love; art. Christina works from home in Los Angeles, California and loves to foster and rescue cats.

Check out the other great titles at: MoonbowPublishing.com